Mr. Croc's Silly Sock

NORTH END

written and illustrated by
Frank Rodgers

PICTURE WINDOW BOOKS
Minneapolis, Minnesota

Editor: Nick Healy
Page Production: Brandie E. Shoemaker
Creative Director: Keith Griffin
Editorial Director: Carol Jones

First American edition published in 2007 by
Picture Window Books
5115 Excelsior Boulevard
Suite 232
Minneapolis, MN 55416
877-845-8392
www.picturewindowbooks.com

First published in 1999 by A&C Black Publishers Limited, 38 Soho Square,
London W1D 3HB, with the title MR CROC'S SILLY SOCK.

Printed in the United States of America.

Library of Congress Cataloging-in-Publication Data
Rodgers, Frank, 1944-
Mr. Croc's silly sock / by Frank Rodgers. — 1st American ed.
p. cm. — (Read-it! chapter books)
Summary: While chasing a runaway sock, a forgetful crocodile pauses to
admire his handsome reflection.
ISBN-13: 978-1-4048-2730-1 (hardcover)
ISBN-10: 1-4048-2730-7 (hardcover)
[1. Crocodiles—Fiction. 2. Animals—Fiction. 3. Memory—Fiction.] I. Title.
II. Title: Mister Croc's silly sock. III. Series.
PZ7.R6154Mrm 2006
[Fic]—dc22   2006003423

EASY
BK

3/16/2007

Table of Contents

Chapter One

Mr. Croc was very busy. It was
Monday, and he was doing
his laundry.

He placed the laundry on the kitchen table and looked out the window. The bushes were swaying in the breeze. "It's very windy today," he said.

He filled the
sink with
hot water,

put in his
dirty clothes,

and added
some soap
from the box.

He sloshed the
water around to
make it sudsy,
but nothing
happened.

7

"That's odd," said Mr. Croc. "Where are all of the bubbles?" He looked at the box and groaned. "No wonder there are no bubbles," he said.

Mr. Croc was very forgetful.

He rinsed the oatmeal off his clothes
and washed them again with
laundry soap.
Next, he put
them through
the wringer to
squeeze
out some of
the water.

Then he took the clothes into the
windy backyard.

"Laundry day is turning out to be harder than usual," said Mr. Croc.

At least my clothes will dry quickly in the wind.

Mr. Croc hung his laundry on the line and watched as it flapped in the breeze.

He was about to go back inside when he noticed something strange.

The laundry was flapping right off the line. "Oh, no!" yelped Mr. Croc.

I forgot to use clothespins!

Mr. Croc ran around the yard,
chasing after his clothes.

After a lot of huffing
and puffing, he
managed to catch
them all.

But as he pinned them back on the
line, he noticed that something was
missing.

Mr. Croc searched all over the yard, but he couldn't find the missing sock. "It must have blown away," he said.

Glumly, he went back into the kitchen. "I need to cheer up," he said.

I know! I'll make a triple-decker sardine sandwich for lunch!

Mr. Croc liked fish. But when he looked in the cupboard, it was empty.

Oh, no! I forgot to buy sardines!

I'll just have to go to the store again.

Mr. Croc put on his jacket and tied his scarf. Then he smiled at himself in the hall mirror. What a lovely smile I've got, he thought.

It cheered him up.

Chapter Two

Mr. Croc headed for the store. He smiled his lovely smile at everyone.

Outside the store, he met his friend Mr. Hound. "Hello, Mr. Croc," said Mr. Hound.

Mr. Croc stopped and scratched his head.

Mr. Croc thought hard. "I think, maybe, it had something to do with socks," he said.

"Socks?" said Mr. Hound. "Funny you should say that."

18

Mr. Croc looked up.

"It's my sock!" replied Mr. Croc.

Mr. Croc reached up to get it.

But as he did, he caught sight
of his reflection in the shop
window. He
stopped and
smiled his
lovely smile.

What a lovely
smile I've got.

Just then, a gust of wind blew the sock onto the arm of the painter, Mr. Gloss.

As he shook it off,
Mr. Gloss dropped
his paint can.

But Mr. Hound
caught it just
in time.

"I'm very sorry, Mr. Gloss," said
Mr. Croc. "It's not really a snake."

The sock sailed off down the street ...

... flipping and flapping in the gusts of wind.

Mr. Croc and Mr. Hound ran after it, huffing and puffing.

Chapter Three

They caught up with the sock at the corner of the street.

It was
dangling
from a
lamppost.

Mr. Croc stretched up to get it.

But as he did so, he saw himself in the side mirror of a parked van.

Mr. Croc smiled a lovely smile.

Just look at all of those lovely teeth!

While Mr. Croc was busy admiring himself, the sock flapped off the lamppost and drifted off.

The sock landed on Mrs. Poodle's nose. She yelped in surprise.

AAAH! I can't see!

She stumbled across the pavement, heading straight for the lamppost.

Mr. Hound stopped her just in time.

"Sorry, Mrs. Poodle," said Mr. Croc.

It's my sock.

It's a very silly sock!

Mrs. Poodle hung the sock on the van's mirror and stomped off.

Mr. Croc reached for the sock.

But the van drove off. ZOOM!

Mr. Croc and Mr. Hound chased
after it.

The van stopped at the traffic light.

But before Mr. Croc could grab the sock, it blew away once again.

The sock knocked Miss Siam's shopping list out of her hands.

The list fluttered in the wind.

Mr. Hound leapt
up and caught it.

"Sorry, Miss Siam," said Mr. Croc.

"Oh, dear," said Mr. Croc as Miss Siam walked off. "My silly sock has caused a lot of trouble. I'd better take it straight home."

Chapter Four

On his way home, Mr. Croc began to wonder what it was he had meant to buy at the store.

But he couldn't remember.

Outside the park, he saw Mr. Gloss, the painter, looking glum. "What's wrong, Mr. Gloss?" asked Mr. Croc.

The wind blew my hat into that holly bush.

And I pricked my fingers trying to rescue it.

Mr. Croc smiled his lovely smile.
"Allow me," he said. He put the sock
over his hand,

reached into the
holly bush, and
pulled out Mr.
Gloss' hat.

Mr. Gloss grinned.
"Good thinking, Mr. Croc," he said.

Thank
you!

As Mr. Croc set off again, he
still wondered about
what he had meant
to buy at the store.

Outside the hairdresser's salon, he
saw Mrs. Poodle. She was standing in
the doorway, and she looked worried.

"What's wrong, Mrs. Poodle?" asked
Mr. Croc.

Mr. Croc smiled his lovely smile.

Carefully, he
placed his sock
over her hair.
The sock made
a very good hat,

and Mrs. Poodle got home with her
new hairdo still in place.

"Good thinking, Mr. Croc," she said.

Thank
you!

Mr. Croc headed
off again, still
wondering about
what he had
meant to buy.

At the corner, he met Miss Siam.
She was looking sadly at her
groceries, which were lying on
the sidewalk.

"What's wrong, Miss Siam?" asked
Mr. Croc.

Miss Siam sighed. "My bag ripped,"
she said.

Mr. Croc smiled his lovely smile and handed Miss Siam his silly sock.

"Why don't you borrow this?" he said. "I've got big feet, so my sock will make a roomy shopping bag."

Miss Siam put all of her groceries in Mr. Croc's sock.

"Good thinking, Mr. Croc," she said.

Thank you. I'll bring it back later.

That's fine, Miss Siam. Bye-bye!

By now, Mr. Croc was nearly home.
But he was still wondering about
what he had meant to buy.

Just then, a bus roared
past. It was full of shoppers.

Mr. Croc gasped.

"Yes!" he cried. "That's it!"

He rushed back to the store.

But he was too late. The store was
closed for the evening.

His tummy rumbled.

Chapter Five

Mr. Croc trudged home feeling very gloomy. But when he got there, he found a surprise waiting for him.

Hanging on his doorknob was
his sock.

Inside were six tins of sardines.

There was also a note.

Dear Mr. Croc,

On my way home, I met Mr. Gloss and Mrs. Poodle. They told me how you had helped them, too. We all know how much you like fish, so here are some sardines—just to say thank you. Enjoy them!

Yours sincerely,
Miss Siam

"Presents in my sock!" cried Mr. Croc. "Wonderful!"

It's just like Christmas!

He took the sock into the kitchen. "Time for food!" he said. But as he unpacked the sardines something caught his eye.

Oops! I forgot all about my laundry, and it has started to rain!

Mr. Croc rushed
outside and
gathered all of
the clothes
from the line.

Then he
ironed them.

He put everything away ...

... except his silly sock.

I suppose I'll have to wash you again!

But you'll have to wait until the next laundry day.

Now it's time for my triple-decker sardine sandwich!

As he opened the tins, Mr. Croc smiled his lovely smile. "All's well that ends well," he said.

Look for More *Read-it!* Chapter Books

Grandpa's Boneshaker Bicycle	978-1-4048-2732-5
Jenny the Joker	978-1-4048-2733-2
Little T and Lizard the Wizard	978-1-4048-2725-7
Little T and the Crown Jewels	978-1-4048-2726-4
Little T and the Dragon's Tooth	978-1-4048-2727-1
Little T and the Royal Roar	978-1-4048-2728-8
The Minestrone Mob	978-1-4048-2723-3
Mr. Croc Forgot	978-1-4048-2731-8
Mr. Croc's Walk	978-1-4048-2729-5
The Peanut Prankster	978-1-4048-2724-0
Silly Sausage and the Little Visitor	978-1-4048-2735-6
Silly Sausage and the Spooks	978-1-4048-2736-3
Silly Sausage Goes to School	978-1-4048-2738-7
Silly Sausage in Trouble	978-1-4048-2737-0
Stan the Dog and the Crafty Cats	978-1-4048-2739-4
Stan the Dog and the Golden Goals	978-1-4048-2740-0
Stan the Dog and the Major Makeover	978-1-4048-2741-7
Stan the Dog and the Sneaky Snacks	978-1-4048-2742-4
Uncle Pat and Auntie Pat	978-1-4048-2734-9

Looking for a specific title? A complete list
of *Read-it!* Chapter Books is available on our Web site:
www.picturewindowbooks.com